getting railed

A Sentient Object Romance

Retro Whimsy
Book One

sabrina cross

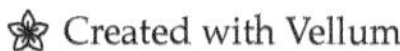 Created with Vellum

author's note

This is a sentient object romance. Humans will be getting it on with sentient objects. Don't worry, everyone is gleefully consenting.

If you read the last three sentences and think that's not for you, that's okay. There is still time to put this book down and walk away. No one will blame you. It's the sane thing to do.

But if you're going to stick around please be aware of the following: vaginal insertion of inanimate objects, oral sex, vaginal sex, anal sex, sex with multiple partners at the same time.

If you feel I am missing anything please reach out to me at authorsabrinacross@gmail.com and let me know. A complete list can be found at www.sabrinacross.com

one

. . .

"Do you think they realize this place is cursed?" My best friend and coworker Cinder asked as we pushed into Old Town's newest store.

"Shhh," I hushed her when a bell rang over the door as it opened, alerting them to our presence. "If they don't know, I don't want to be the one to tell them."

I wasn't sure how they couldn't know. The building was a gorgeous, freestanding light brick storefront on the edges of Old Town. It was prime real estate with lots of foot traffic in a cute and kitschy part of town that was often busy. But for some reason, no matter what type of business opened there, they never lasted. The record for going under was set at just six weeks for a yarn store that caught fire and burnt half the inventory before they got it out.

The building had been a number of things in the ten years since I started working in Old Town. There had been a tea shop that got busted for selling psychotropic herbal blends. It'd been a kid's salon, a hot dog shop, a wreath store, and a craft collective. We'd thought the bookstore had a fighting chance, but then the owners closed the doors one day without notice and were never heard from or seen again.

The store was cute. It was an open space with little alcoves made of shelving units. The wide center was split in half with free-standing racks overflowing with vintage clothing. An L-shaped glass display made up the counter near the front of the store where the woman was sorting through a large cardboard box of things.

The woman working the store was as interesting as anything in there. She was probably in her late thirties with brown hair cut in a smart short style that framed icy blue eyes. She was stunning in a pair of bronze wide-legged, high-waisted pants and a white button-down shirt with a mandarin collar.

She caught me staring at her from halfway across the store and winked. I had a moment of panic and whirled around to grab the first thing off of the shelf nearest me, as if I wasn't totally caught staring. Gosh, I was such a weirdo.

"Oh hey, I used to have that as a kid!" Cinder said, taking the toy from my hand. It was an ugly little plastic thing with fuzzy green hair standing about as tall as the doll itself. I happily relinquished it, having always been terrified of the things with their giant, empty eyes and soul-stealing expression.

I left her to the dolls and continued wandering. I checked my watch, fifteen more minutes on our lunch break. We'd have to head out soon. Our office wasn't far from the heart of Old Town but we tended to stroll and meander rather than speed walk. Especially when it was hot out and the risk of wilting in the heat was real.

"Can I help you find anything?" The cheery voice behind me had me nearly jumping out of my skin. I whirled around to see the woman only a few feet away. She had been completely silent crossing the store. I hadn't heard her coming.

"We're just wandering," I said, hand to my chest as I willed my heart to slow.

"You wandered in for a reason," her smile was saccharin. She eyed me up and down before snapping her fingers. "I bet I know just the thing to interest you."

"No, really. I'm not shopping today." Politeness propelled me to follow her as she headed with determined steps to the very back of the store. "We just saw a new store and wanted to check it out."

"Here we are." She bent over and picked up a large wood crate from the bottom of a shelf covered in tin cars. "This is for you."

The crate was shoved into my arms and I looked down at a train set. There were neat piles of plastic and wire rails on top of which sat what looked to be two or three trains worth of cars.

"No," I tried to shove the crate back at her, but she took a smiling step backward. "I'm sorry but I honestly have no use for this."

"Are you sure?" With another wink, she turned and walked back to the front of the store. I watched her and wondered what the fuck I was supposed to do with a toy train set.

I didn't even notice Cinder's arrival at my side until she grabbed the edge of the crate and tilted it so she could look inside.

"Hey Aubry we've gotta get back. Oh, Is this for Parker? It'd be perfect for him!" I blinked up at my friend and then shook my head, still confused by the interaction I'd just had.

"Parker?" I knew she meant my nephew, but I couldn't imagine what he had to do with the moment.

"Yeah? Isn't his birthday coming up?"

Oh, right. He was turning the big six in a few weeks. I'd mentioned needing to find him something suitably awesome. I glanced down at the train set in my arms. He'd never expressed an undue interest in trains before, but it was just the kind of thing he'd like.

"Yeah. That's right. It's for Parker." I nodded once and then started toward the front of the shop. Cinder fell into step beside me. "Find anything interesting?"

"Nah." She glanced over her shoulder toward something, but then just shook her head. "I don't think so."

two

· · ·

When I got home, I hauled the crate of trains up the three stories to my apartment, still wondering how I'd gotten talked into buying them. What was worse, I had to set everything up first to test it was working before I could gift it to my nephew. No way was I going to be the aunt that got him a dud toy.

"Later," I promised myself as I set the crate down on the table and stretched my back. First, I would shower, pour myself a glass of wine, and change into some comfy clothes. Not necessarily in that order.

Thirty minutes later, I padded barefoot into my living room wearing a pair of loose shorts and a crop tank with my wet hair clipped up. Once upon a time, spending Friday night alone in my apartment would have horrified me. Now, at thirty-four, I was more than comfortable with my own company. Especially when the alternative was yet another date from some fuckboy from a dating app. No, thank you.

I set my bottle of white wine and a clean glass on the end table and propped my hands on my hips as I eyed the crate and my living room. From what I could remember from playing with train sets as a kid, they didn't do well on carpet. But everywhere in my apartment besides the bathroom was carpeted. There was no way that it would fit on the small space-saving table tucked away in my kitchen.

"Floor it is and we'll just hope for the best," I muttered, grabbing the crate and moving it to the floor. I poured myself a glass of wine and thought vaguely about ordering some food before starting to assemble the tracks.

"Trains first, food later." If worse came to worse, I could always just pop a bag of microwave popcorn and call it a night. Everyone knew wine and popcorn was a top tier girl dinner.

It took me over an hour to assemble the track. I had not expected the winding path that crossed over itself at least three times before returning the train to the station. Once it was finally set up, I poured myself a second glass of wine and sat back on the carpet with the trains themselves. There were three trains. Each train had an engine, compartment, and caboose. They hooked together with a little peg and loop that allowed them to twist and turn along the track; I supposed. The fit was loose, and it made getting the completed train onto the track difficult.

To make matters more annoying, the little power toggle was located on the bottom of the engine. Which meant you had to turn the thing over, reattach it to the rest of the train, and get it on the track. Such a terrible design.

Amazingly, all three trains turned on when I flipped the switch. The little wheels began to turn as I reassembled the train and set it on the track.

Before long, I had three trains seamlessly circling the track that took up much of my living room.

There was a surge of satisfaction as I watched the trains circle the tracks. The low hum of them was a satisfying, steady sound in the background as I made myself dinner, popcorn and wine, and settled in on the couch with my e-reader.

I hadn't planned on getting turned on by a book about a demon teddy bear, but I couldn't deny the tension building in my body. I slid my hand inside my panties to idly cup my pussy. When the teddy-turned-demon started stalking the FMC through the house in a mask, I started wishing I had charged my vibrator after the last use.

The sound of the trains on the track met me, and I looked over at them. They had vibrated quite a bit in my hand when I had turned them on.

No. No. It was insane.

My pussy fluttered and clenched on nothing as my fingers circled my clit. It felt good, but not good enough. I needed more.

"I cannot believe I'm about to do this." I rolled off the couch and crossed to grab one of the trains. The green one was nearest to me. I grabbed it off the track and held it upside down in my hand. The vibration was nice and steady and just what I needed.

"No way I can give you to Parker now," I said, returning to my spot on the couch and picking up my e-reader. I spread my legs and propped one up against the back of the couch while the other foot was planted on the floor. The train was still running in my hand.

I disconnected the engine from the cars and dropped the cars to the floor before eyeing the humming engine. Was I really about to do this? My pussy fluttered and, fuck it, yeah, I was.

I returned to my book and idly traced the train across my chest and teased my nipples. As things escalated with the demon teddy bear, I traced the train down my sternum, over the curve of my belly.

"Last chance not to be a total weirdo," I told myself, already shoving the leg of my loose shorts aside to give myself access. The train was a bullet-shaped toy with four spinning wheels. It was about two inches tall and seven inches long. While the vibration wasn't anywhere near as hard as a vibrator, it was a nice steady hum that was going to feel so good on my thrumming clit.

Giving in, I pressed the train upside down to my slit. It buzzed pleasantly, but it wasn't nearly enough. I pushed it down until the train lay directly on my clit and gasped. I was already wet and throbbing and the vibration felt nice. It probably wouldn't be enough to get me off, but it was enough to wind me up as I read.

When the spicy scene finished, I dropped the e-reader to the floor and focused on my own rising need. I angled the train, looking for more vibration, but it just wasn't enough. I was empty and aching. After the barest of hesitation, I flicked the switch on the train to turn off the motor.

"This is a bad idea," I muttered. Knowing it was a bad idea wasn't enough to stop me from moving the train to my entrance. It wasn't very wide, but it was long and I was horny. I eased the train into me, gently fucking myself with the plastic toy.

I moaned, thrusting up into my hand as I drove the toy as deep as I dared to go and still keep a steady grip on it. I mean, I wasn't shoving it up my ass or anything, but I did not want to end up in the emergency room with a toy train shoved up my vagina.

It had to be the most depraved thing I'd ever done, but there was no stopping. I was racing full steam ahead toward orgasm. I thrust the train in and out of my tunnel, moaning at the sensation. At some point, I flipped the little switch and the wheels started to turn. It provided a strange sensation that sent me flying into orgasm.

I pulled the train free. It was coated in my cream and sticky to the touch. Then it got weird. The train started heating and shaking in my hand. A bright light flashed. I dropped the train to cover my eyes.

When I uncovered them, I was no longer alone. There was a man in my living room. A naked man. A hard, naked man. A large, hard, naked man. A hot, large, hard, naked man.

"What the fuck?"

three

. . .

"At last!" The man dropped to his knees next to the couch. I pulled my own knees to my chest and wrapped my legs around them as he crowded close. "My angel, you have rescued me!"

He reached out a hand, but I flinched away. He leaned back and eyed me for a moment before looking around the room.

"Where are the others?" His dark brows drew together over dark eyes. His face matched his body, both lean and long. His torso rippled with muscles as he twisted to look at the two trains still circling the track.

"Others?" I followed his gaze to the track and dawning horror settled over me. "There are others?"

"There are three of us." He got to his feet and crossed to the tracks. I couldn't keep my eyes off his tight ass as he bent to pick up the other trains. He disconnected the cars and cradled them in his large hands. "Why didn't they come back?"

Because I didn't fuck them. The words were on the tip of my tongue, but it was too much. Too fucking much. I wasn't exactly sure what was happening, but I had not summoned a hot guy by fucking a toy train. I hadn't. Because that would be insane.

"Look, I'm not sure who you are or why you're here but how about you leave and I'll pretend this never happened and won't call the cops? You can even take the trains if they mean that much to you." I got up and reached for my phone on the side table.

"You released me. You must be able to release them." His eyebrows drew together again as he looked at the trains, then me, then back to the trains. "You have to take them inside of your body."

"Actually no, I don't."

"You took me." His teeth flashed in a grin. "It did not appear to be a problem for you to do so. You seemed to greatly enjoy it. I could help you do it again. We must release Leo and Markus."

"Look buddy, I don't known what game you're playing here but I'm not fucking any more toy trains. That was a moment of insanity." I held the phone in my hand, unsure of what to do. Calling the cops would have made the most sense, but what if he tried to tell them he had been a train until five minutes ago? How could I explain that? Because as crazy as it sounded, I really did suspect he had been the train.

I was clearly losing my mind. I'd gone insane that morning and no one had thought to tell me. It was the only reason I could think of for buying a train set I didn't want and then violating one of those trains in a moment of frustrated horniness. Never once in my life had I been so horny I'd fucked a non-body safe item, and yet there we were.

"Please, you have to help them." He came closer,

and I stepped back and to the side, putting a chair between us.

"No, I don't think I do." I gripped my phone in one hand and the back of the chair with the other. I wished there was something nearby to use as a weapon, though I didn't feel particularly threatened. Yes, he was large, and naked, and aroused, but I didn't feel like I was in danger or anything.

"We cannot leave them like this. You're the only one who can help them." He held the trains out in his large hands and I eyed them. The engines were still running, their little wheels spinning endlessly as he held them upside down.

Were there men trapped in those trains? Did I believe that? How would that even happen? It was too crazy to contemplate, but I didn't know what else to think. I was pretty sure he was a train five minutes ago. And if that was true, it was possible the other trains could turn into men.

"How?" I shifted on my feet. I felt a little silly standing there with the chair between us and my phone clasped in my hand if I wasn't going to use it. "How is this possible?"

"Do you believe in magic?" The man said after a long pause.

"In a young girl's heart?" Confusion wrinkled his face, and he shook his head.

"No, real magic. Witches and gods and curses?" I shifted to lean against the side of the recliner. I refused to sit and give him the edge should he decide to attack me.

"Not in the slightest." I wasn't big on anything I couldn't see or touch. But my worldview felt like it was expanding by the second.

"We were cursed. Got caught with our pants

down with the wrong woman and the god of love didn't much care for us defiling his daughter," he sounded almost apologetic with that absurd statement. Almost.

"Uh-huh," I reached forward to grab my bottle of wine off the table and took a swig. "So you fucked a god and got turned into a toy train? And what, just magically appeared in my living room? Sure, that's totally logical."

"We didn't fuck the god, we fucked his daughter." He said it like this was a perfectly reasonable thing to say.

"Isn't a god's daughter, by default, also a god?" Yeah, yeah, I had a Greek Mythology obsession like every other weird girl in middle school.

"Not always, it's complicated," he waved it away like he wasn't trying to single-handedly upend my entire understanding of mythology. And why was I listening like any of this was real and he wasn't handing me a line of total bullshit?

"Uh-huh," I took another deep swig of wine. Maybe alcohol would make this make sense because logic wasn't having anything to do with it. "So anyway, you fucked a god's daughter, the three of you together? Wow. Okay. So, anyway, Daddy God got pissed and turned you into toy trains?"

"No. He cursed us to be figurines. I'm not exactly sure when or why we were turned into toys. That's not important."

He stepped forward. My eyes drew downward to his bobbing cock that still stood at attention. Wasn't that uncomfortable? I snapped my gaze to the ceiling and took another drink.

"I think it's pretty important. It seems important," I took another drink and met his gaze. "What do I have to do with any of this?"

"You picked us." The man said. "You chose us out of all of them and you brought us into your home. You took me into your body and accepted me. You're the one who can break our curse."

"Curse broken. You can go on and find someone else to free your friends." I waved him off toward the front door.

"That's not possible." He dropped down onto the couch and I took that as a sign I could drop into the chair. Which was good, given how shaky my legs felt. "It has to be you."

If all it took to break the curse was to fuck a train, there were plenty of kinky women out there ready and willing. Especially if asked by someone who looked like that guy. He was over six feet, lean, with abs that gave way to that V at his hips directing attention to his dick. That was before you got to his face, sharp features framed by long golden brown hair and dark blue eyes that drilled into you.

No, it wouldn't be hard for him to find someone else willing to fuck his train buddies back to human form. So why did it have to be me?

"We were all cursed to the same fate. Which means the curse can only be broken in the same way by the same person." He stared at me, his eyes intense and pleading. "I'm not sure how long I'll maintain this form if you don't help Leo and Markus. Please, beauty, help us."

He held out the trains to me again. The sane part of my mind was screaming to get him out of my apartment and slam the door. Lock him out and pretend the whole thing never happened. It was absurd and no one would believe me anyway.

But there was something about him. Something about the sad, broken look in his eyes that had me second guessing myself. I wanted to help him. I wanted to erase that look from his eyes.

"Tell me what we have to do."

four

. . .

$\mathscr{H}$is entire face lit up like the fourth of July. The lines surrounding his eyes and mouth faded, and his muscles relaxed. It was like watching a wave travel over his body, leaving relief in its path.

"You have to take them into your body." He held them out for me, as if to shove them up my cunt that moment.

"Do I have to fuck them? Wouldn't putting them in my mouth do it?" As gross as the idea of sticking the old toys into my mouth was, I really wasn't interested in messing up my vagina PH balance any more than I already had. Oh my god, what I had I been thinking fucking that toy? I hadn't even washed it off first. Who knew how many people had touched it or how long it'd been sitting in storage.

"I don't know. The curse wasn't very clear. Just that our three fates were intertwined. It wasn't made to be broken. When a god curses you, they tend to want you to stay that way."

"How do I know you don't deserve to be cursed? Maybe he had a good reason to turn you into toys." The thought struck me suddenly that maybe he was a rapist and deserved every moment he spent as a toy, and that releasing his friends might free more rapists.

Something of my thoughts must have shown on my face, because the man recoiled with a look of horror on his face. His wide eyes flew to mine, and he shook his head. He lifted a hand to touch me but dropped it like I'd burned him.

"My friends and I have never forced ourselves on anyone. We've never had to. The girl was an enthusiastic partner in our bed sport. Had we known who she was, we would have never touched her. But she came to us, not the other way around. I, we would never hurt you."

Again, I couldn't explain why, but I believed him. There was something about him I wanted to trust. Maybe it was just the fact that I'd been alone for so long, but I didn't want him to be the bad guy in this story.

"Okay, but are we sure I can't just lick them?" I finally took the trains from him. They were still running, the little wheels spinning uselessly. Now that the edge had been taken off, the idea of fucking myself with them was pretty insane and not at all appealing. I turned the trains off and set them in my lap.

"I don't know if I can do this," I admitted. I couldn't meet the man's eyes as I toyed with my fingers and considered the trains.

"Let me help you," He slid off the couch to his knees and crawled to me. His eyes were intent on mine as he stopped a breath away from me. "I can help make it good for you," he grinned, the smile slightly lopsided. "It's the least I can do."

My stomach dropped. Was he suggesting I was

a pity fuck? That he felt obligated to fuck me so I would help his friends?

"No need. I'll just pull up some smut or something. I'd hate to put you out." My voice was cool, and a line developed between his drawn brows.

"You think you'd be putting me out?" His hand came up to grab my chin. He used his grip to force me to meet his gaze. "You think I'm not dying to get my hands on the plump curves of you? That my cock doesn't weep at the thought of sinking inside of that sweet cunt as a man? I want to fuck you in every position we can think. You are far from a burden."

My breath caught in my chest and the bright intensity in his eyes held me hostage. Before I could think any better of it, I wrapped my hand around the back of his neck and dragged his mouth to mine.

He groaned into my mouth and released my face. His hands moved to my knees and his tongue invaded my mouth. I gripped his hair and held as he devoured me. He used his grip on my knees to spread my legs and settled himself between them. His hands slid up the outside of my thighs to my hips and he gripped.

I gasped when he yanked me forward and brought my core against his bare torso. My shorts rode up and left my legs and part of my ass bare.

"You taste so good," he groaned into my mouth. A thought struck me and I jerked back.

"What do I call you? What's your name?" I was half naked and making out with a man and didn't even know his name. My nanna would be rolling over in her grave.

"Julian," he moved his mouth to my neck and

my head lolled back to give him more room. "What do I call you?"

Anything you want so long as you keep doing that. I bit back the words and gasped out my name as his lips sealed over the soft hollow behind my ear at the same time his hands moved to cup my breasts.

"You taste divine, Aubry. I cannot wait to fuck you. But first," he picked up one of the trains from where they fell to the floor.

I eyed the train, a little disappointed. Kissing him had been so good, I lost my mind. And he was still just thinking about his friends. He must have picked up on my disappointment because his hands fisted in my hair and his mouth crashed back down to mine. The kiss was hard, deep, and demanding.

"Don't worry, dove. I will not leave you wanting. My friends and I will take care of you."

His mouth returned to mine. He sat the train down again and gripped my ass with both hands. I moaned when he used his grip to rub my pussy against his torso. The ridges of his abs provided friction against my damp flesh. My shorts clung to my wet folds, and I wished they were off.

Julian obviously agreed, because he pulled away with a growl. He released my ass to grab my waistband and pull the shorts down my thighs. I lifted my butt to help him.

"So pretty," Julian said as he eyed my pink petals. He ran a finger down my slit and toyed with the dampness gathered at my opening. My body clenched on nothing, and I nearly whined when he pulled away.

My disappointment was short-lived. Julian dipped his head and replaced his finger with his tongue. He lapped at me in long strokes from opening to clit. His low groan vibrated against me and my hands flew to bury in his hair.

My hips rose to meet his mouth. His lips closed around my clit. My hands tugged at his hair as I forced his face against my pussy. Tension curled in my belly. Julian licked, flicked, and sucked my clit and had me seeing stars.

A wide, blunt finger slid inside of me and ratcheted up my pleasure. It was quickly replaced with two fingers that curled and flexed inside of me. Julian scissored them gently, spreading me wide.

I couldn't stop the whine that escaped when he removed his fingers. I was so close it almost hurt.

"Shh, dove. It's time. I want to feel you come all over Leo." He picked up the blue train and pressed it against my opening. His mouth returned to my clit as he guided the toy inside of me.

The train was off and lacked the slight vibration of the first time. While I noted the loss, I couldn't complain. Not with Julian's lips closed around my clit in deep, satisfying pulls.

I couldn't keep still. My hips thrust up against the toy and his mouth. Pleasure pooled in my belly and made my legs shake.

"Please," I begged, unsure what I was asking for. Just something more. Some relief. "Please."

Julian didn't respond with words. He hummed against me before switching his grip on the train. Gone were the slow strokes and steady pulls. Julian devoured me as he fucked me with the train. My fingers dug into the arms of the chair as I struggled to absorb all of the sensations flowing through me.

"Yes, fuck, yes!" My body exploded and stars danced behind my eyes as my body clenched down on the train.

"That's it, dove." Julian stared up at me as my body spasmed. "Come for me."

I could do nothing but obey as he kept up the erratic thrusts of the train inside of me. He didn't stop until I came down and my body went limp.

Julian lifted the train to his mouth and I watched through slitted eyes as he licked my cream off the toy. It was utterly filthy and made my pussy clench.

"You taste so sweet." Julian set the train aside and wrapped a hand around my neck. He pulled me forward and to him until his mouth crashed into mine. I could taste my cum on his tongue and the musky flavor added to my pleasure. The man ate pussy like it was his last meal.

"My turn." Julian said against my mouth. It was the only warning I had before Julian gripped my hips and pulled me off the chair and down until I straddled his hips. His hard cock was hot between my legs.

He pulled me with him as he laid back against the carpet, allowing his dick to slide between my folds. He thrust up against me and bumped the head of his cock against my clit.

"Ride me, dove."

I didn't need to be told twice.

five

. . .

ulian's cock was hard and hot in my hand as I rose up over him. It took seconds to line him up at my opening. His fingers flexed at my hips as I slowly slid down his length. I was sensitive from my previous orgasms and so tight. The press of him was a satisfying burn as I continued my slow descent down his cock.

"That's it, dove You're taking me so well." Julian applied slight pressure to my hips, dragging me further down his shaft until my hips were flush with his. He wasn't particularly long but he was wide and the stretch felt so good.

I gripped his thighs and slid the rest of the way down. I settled there and let myself adjust. It was only a moment though before Julian used his grip on my hips to encourage me to start moving. Before too long, I was bouncing on his dick like a pogo stick.

"Is this a private ride or can anyone climb aboard?"

I screamed and slammed down hard at the voice coming from behind me. I had forgotten about the other train already.

My hands flew to cover my tits and I tried to dismount Julian but his grip on my hips wouldn't let me move. I sat there frozen, astride Julian, and unsure of what to do.

"What do you think, dove? Are you up for another?" The other man came into view. He was tall, easily six-five. His skin was pale and he was more broad than Julian. His hair was a light fawn brown that matched his eyes. His body wasn't as sculpted as Julian's but it wasn't soft either. His cock was already hard. It was shorter but wider than Julian's, who was already stretching me to the max. I wasn't even sure I could take a cock that wide.

But I was game to try.

Maybe it was my years-long dry spell. Maybe it was all of the smutty books I'd been reading lately. Maybe deep down I was just a massive slut begging to come out and play. Whatever the reason, I wanted both of these strangers and I wanted them inside of me now.

"Leo, meet Aubry, she's the one who freed us." Julian thrust up into me and I bit back a moan at the movement. "Aubry, meet Leo. He's going to fuck your face now."

Before I could even say hello, Leo was standing over Julian's head with his cock at eye level with my mouth. He grinned down at me and caught a hand in my hair at the back of my head.

"Pinch me if it's too much," his voice was faintly accented but I couldn't place it. And then he was sliding his giant cock into my mouth and thoughts of accents and strangers went out the window at the salty taste of him.

Julian continued to move me over his cock while Leo held me in place and fed me his dick. It was absolutely filthy and hedonistic and overwhelming. My jaw ached, my pussy clenched hard on Julian's dick. Both men were moaning and groaning as they used my body for their pleasure. I dug my hands into Leo's thighs and held on as the head of his cock slid to the back of my mouth and tried to push into my throat. It was too much. It was all too much.

I screamed around the dick in my mouth as I clenched down on the one in my pussy. I came so hard, harder than I'd ever come in my life. Julian sped up his thrusts, following me over the edge. Leo pulled free of my mouth, still hard, and helped ease me down to rest against Julian's chest.

"Such a good little dove, thank you." Julian's words were soft against my shoulder as he stroked my back.

Leo knelt down beside us, his hand joined Julian's on my back. Their touch was reverent as they stroked and petted me.

"You took me so well, lamb. I'm so proud of you." I arched under their touch and praise. "Where's Markus?"

"Over there somewhere," Julian's hand abandoned me to wave in the direction of the chair. "We haven't gotten to him yet."

"Probably smart." Leo said, his hand slid even lower on my back to the curve of my ass. "He's kind of a grumpy ass."

"Mmm," I hum against Julian's neck, utterly boneless under their caressing hands.

"Oh, he's not that bad," Julian says. He grabbed both my hips again and moved me over his slowly hardening cock. I let out a little whimper as sensation flooded my oversensitive clit.

"Careful Julian, don't wear her out just yet."

Leo's fingers dipped between my cheeks to tease my hole.

"Need me to rescue your friend?" The words felt bitter on my tongue.

"No, little lamb. I haven't had my turn yet and, while your mouth is damn near heaven, I want to feel you come around my cock. We'll get to Markus when we get to him."

Julian used his legs to spread mine wide. He pulled his knees up and grasped my thighs. The position left my holes completely exposed for Leo's exploring fingers. I thought that was the point at first.

"Don't be an ass. Get Markus. You'll get your chance after she turns him back." Julian pressed a kiss to the top of my head. "You can take it, can't you dove?"

To be honest, I wasn't sure if I could. I'd already come multiple times and my pussy was tight and tender. But I'd promised to help Julian and his friends and I didn't want to let him down. I nodded into Julian's chest and just tried to relax. Julian's hands stroked along my legs to my ass and back down to my knees. Leo's fingers teased and stroked my sensitive slit. Julian's cum provided lubrication as he sank a finger inside of me but I couldn't stop myself from tensing up.

"Shh, it's okay lamb," Leo's voice was soft and gentle as he stroked his finger inside of me. "I won't do anything that doesn't feel good. Just relax and let us take care of you."

Julian started kissing a path on my neck, muttering praise the whole time. His hands continued to stroke my back and arms in long, sweeping gestures that soothed me even as Leo's finger continued to work me up. He pulled out and returned with two fingers. This time his thumb pressed against my ass as he flexed and curled his fingers inside of me.

I'd done some ass play in the past but it had never been my favorite thing. Now, I realized it had been more about comfort with my partner than discomfort with the act. When Leo's thumb pressed past the tight ring, I couldn't help but arch my back.

"So responsive," Leo cooed at me and curled his fingers to press down on the spot on my lower wall that drove me out of my mind. "You're going to be so beautiful taking us all."

His thumb pressed deeper and I let out a low moan that made Julian chuckle beneath me and gently sink his teeth into my neck. I could feel his cock, rock hard, between my splayed labia. How was he already hard again?

I bit my lips against a whine when Leo removed his fingers from inside of me. They both seemed to sense it though because Julian's hand tangled in my hair and he pulled me in for a kiss even as Leo began muttering reassurances from behind me.

"Don't worry, little lamb, you'll get what you need. First, I'm going to use this train on you so you can free Markus. Then I'm going to fuck you senseless. When I'm all done, Markus will kiss you all better. Would you like that?"

I couldn't answer with Julian's tongue in my mouth but I nodded anyway. Yes, impossibly, ridiculously yes. I wanted all of it so badly. I had never been a multiple orgasms girl but apparently it was more the company I'd kept than a physical ability. Sure, I could get myself off a couple of times with a solid vibrator but this was the first time I'd had anyone spend this much time on my pleasure.

Julian's hands slid down to my ass and he

gripped the large globes, spreading me wide. I felt the cool plastic press against my opening and I braced for penetration. What I didn't even know to brace for was the wet swipe of Leo's tongue on my backdoor. I jerked at the warm, wet touch but Julian's hands held me in place.

"Nothing that won't make you feel good." He muttered against my mouth before sliding back in with another deep, drugging kiss.

I was so tangled up in the strange new sensation of Leo's mouth, I hardly noticed when the train slid inside of me. That was, until Leo started moving it in time with the laps of his tongue. I was tight and sensitive enough I could feel the wheels as the train rolled in and out of me.

One of Julian's hands abandoned my ass and moved between us to cup and knead at my breast. He rolled a nipple between nimble fingers and pinched lightly. The slight pain had me gasping into his mouth. There were too many sensations and they started blending together as the men continued to touch, stroke, kiss, and fuck me. It didn't take long for me to become a writhing, moaning mess. I had to stop kissing Julian as their hands and tongues brought me to the edge. I was letting out a near constant stream of moans and whimpers and pleas.

"Stop, I need– Please. I just, I can't." I wasn't even sure what I was begging for at that point. I just knew something inside me was about to break and I was terrified if it did; I would never be the same again.

"It's okay, dove. You're nearly there. You can do this. Just let go. Leo and I will catch you." Julian's hand tangled into my hair and yanked me until I met his dark gaze. "We won't let you fall alone.

You've been so good for us, so strong. Just let go. Come for us."

I shattered. My body clamped down on the train and I went flying. I swear I saw stars as the pleasure that had been building inside of me exploded. The train was yanked out of my body and I was immediately filled again as Leo slid his cock inside of my spasming vagina.

While the train hadn't been very large, Leo filled my tunnel to the max. He worked himself inside of me and held. I was still riding the edge of pleasure when he started moving. His hands moved to my hips and he held me in place while he thrust into me. The movement pushed me down onto Julian's cock, which was still pressed between my lips.

Every one of Leo's movements drove my clit into Julian's shaft. I was so overstimulated that I didn't know how to tell one sensation from another. My entire body was shaking between the two men. And when Leo bent over me to wrap a hand around Julian's mouth to pull him in for a kiss, I lost it.

I clamped down on Leo's broad cock so hard he swore and pulled away from Julian. I wanted to apologize for breaking up their kiss but I wasn't capable of anything but screaming my pleasure as the two men moved together. I felt Julian's cock begin to spasm below me just before the first hot jet of his cum burst out to cover my belly. Leo roared behind me as he thrust deep and held. The two men worked in tandem to fill and cover me with cum.

I was still working on coming down from what had to be the best orgasm of my life when I heard a new voice. It was low and gravely, he had a faint mediterranean accent.

"My turn."

six

. . .

mewled in protest when Leo pulled out of me. I could feel his cum trail out of my body and coat Julian's balls beneath me. It didn't seem to bother him to have another man's cum on his testicles though, so I didn't comment on it.

Not that I could. I was boneless and speechless.

"Give her a moment, Markus." Julian said, gently stroking my back. I felt more than saw Leo get up and walk away. I was insensible, boneless, helpless.

"She can have all the time she needs."

I turned my head to the side to see the last toy turned man. He was a giant. He was the shortest of the three, but he was big. Everywhere. His arms and thighs were impossibly thick, his chest broad, his belly slightly rounded. And his cock was a goddamn tree branch jutting from between his legs. That last fact broke me.

"I'm done." I murmured into Julian's neck. "Can't."

Julian's hand came up to cup the back of my neck. His grip was firm and comforting. He pressed a kiss to my temple.

"Nothing you don't want, remember. Rest. We'll take care of you." His words were a low comfort.

The new man, Markus, came to sit beside us. He picked up a strand of my hair and twirled it around his finger. My eyes fluttered shut as he untangled himself and brushed my hair back from my face. Leo returned with a warm cloth and cleaned Julian and I up.

A warm blanket draped over me. Rough hands continued stroking my back and the hair from my face. I was boneless and exhausted. I'd never felt more cared for before in my life. I was drifting in the liminal space between sleep and consciousness when Markus spoke.

"They picked well," he said, as he finger combed the tangles from my hair.

"Better than you could imagine," Leo said.

I thought his hands were the ones massaging my lower back.

"They who?" I mumbled. Forming words was a struggle in my exhausted state.

"Rest, pet. We'll talk when you awaken." Markus' fingers dug into my scalp in massaging circles. I had no choice but to obey.

I WOKE up on the couch, snuggled on someone's lap. My legs were propped on someone else's lap and they were idly massaging my calves. I shifted and felt the hard cock beneath me twitch in response. How? How was anyone still hard?

My entire body ached. I could feel my pulse between my legs. Every muscle was sore, like running a marathon without training. Not that I'd ever run a marathon. My ass didn't run unless someone was chasing me.

"Are you back with us?" The question made the chest I was leaning against vibrate. It was so tempting to just keep my eyes closed and sink back into the warmth and go back to sleep. But, I'd unleashed three large men and needed to deal with that.

"Kinda." I worked one of my arms free of the blanket and pushed my hair back from my face. It wasn't nearly as crazy as I'd expected, but then I remembered the feel of someone's fingers detangling it as I'd drifted off.

"How long was I out?" I asked, opening my eyes at last. I was still laying on Julian's lap with my legs slung over Leo's. Markus sat in the chair near us. All three men were still completely, unabashedly, naked.

"Less than an hour," Leo said. He offered me a smile and pat on the thigh.

The blanket over me was half on the floor and only covering my lap. I grabbed it and wrapped myself in the soft material. I internally cringed at the idea of these men seeing me naked and asleep.

"Okay, so," I struggled to find my composure and dignity while I sat on a strange man's lap wearing nothing but a blanket. "You're all back. Perfect. Enjoy your lives."

"It's not that simple." Julian said. He ran his hand through his dark hair, muscles flexing with the movement. He glanced at the others before looking down at me. "It won't last. You chose us, but you have to accept us for it to last. Otherwise, in forty-eight hours we'll be back in the trains and stuck waiting for the next person."

"Accept you how?" I didn't want to know. Deep

in my stomach, I knew deep down I did not want the answer to my question. So, of course, Markus had to answer it.

"We have to fuck you, and you have to like it." He grinned at me, but it wasn't a cheerful or comforting look. It was the look of a predator about to catch its prey. "Don't worry, pet. You'll like it."

seven

. . .

"And on that note, I'm done. Y'all have good luck with the whole curse thing. I'm going to bed." I struggled my way off of Julian's lap and down the hall. I'd already gone farther with these men than I'd ever gone with someone I hadn't been dating for weeks. Now that I wasn't trapped in the insanity of lust, I couldn't believe what I'd done.

A hand wrapped around my waist, and I was pulled back against a wide, hard body. The hand was huge, spanning much of my wide, soft, belly. I knew without looking it was Markus. If the hand hadn't given him away, the tree limb digging into my lower back definitely would have.

He curved around me so he could whisper in my ear. "Sweetheart, we'll make it so good for you, you'll forget every man that came before us. We'll fuck you so well you'll feel us everywhere for days until you're begging us to do it again."

He pressed a kiss to the side of my neck, warm and open mouthed. It had me swaying back against him. It'd been a long time since I'd bothered to try dating. It wasn't him. It was a physical reaction to stimuli. An extreme reaction, but just a basic body response.

I opened my eyes and Leo was standing in front of me, his golden eyes bright on my face. He took a step forward and ran a finger across my collar bone.

"We won't make you do anything you don't want," Leo said, sliding his hand down my sternum to stop just above Marcus' hand on my bare belly. He toyed with the edges of the blanket. "We won't pressure you. But you're the only chance we have. We've waited centuries for this."

A third body joined the group and Julian was suddenly there at my shoulder. He cupped my face in his hand and turned me to face him. I was completely surrounded by them now. At five-two and two-hundred pounds, I wasn't insubstantial. But they were all so big I felt overwhelmed by them.

It was insane. All of them were tall, gorgeous, and built. They could get any girl they wanted at any time. And, from the sound of it, were used to getting them. The idea of them picking me, outside of this weird curse, was absurd.

I had grown to love my body. I wasn't skinny, I wasn't the right kind of curvy. I was plump and rounded and best described as cute. Men like this did not go for cute. And while I felt bad for them, if what they said was true, I wasn't going to let myself be used.

Julian leaned down to brush his lips against mine and I pulled away. I slid out of the group and pressed my back against the wall with the hand not clutching the blanket in front of me.

It was insane. The whole thing was insane.

The three of them stayed just out of reach, their faces ranged from hopeful to angry. The sane part of my brain was yelling at me to run. I'd already had the best sex of my life with two of them. They could find someone else to fuck the curse away. It wouldn't be hard.

But it had been over a year since my last disastrous attempt at dating when the guy had gotten me naked and then decided he couldn't do the fat girl after all. Maybe it was just the magic from the curse, but I had three impossibly attractive men standing in front of me with hard cocks and they wanted to fuck me.

My pussy was practically screaming at me to spread my legs and let them use me. It was an incredibly stupid idea. Terrible. But maybe there was a way to help them and get me what I wanted too.

"Please Aubry," Leo said, eyes pleading. "Help us."

eight

. . .

"**S**o, I just have to sleep with you and you'll turn back into men full time and that's it?"

All three men nodded once. It seemed too easy.

"And this isn't some sort of mating ceremony and I'll be stuck with you forever if we do this?"

Markus looked amused, but the other two assured me it wasn't a mating ceremony and there would be no permanent bond.

"God curses are terrible but they tend to take their ire out on people who deserve it." Julian assured me.

"All of Greek mythology calls you a liar," I told him. He raised an eyebrow at me but didn't say anything else. "This doesn't have to be an all at once thing, does it? Because I don't know if I'm okay with that."

The three men looked at each other and slowly shook their heads. Not a single one of them looked convincing for a moment. My stomach clenched. There was a lot of penis in front of me and I had a pretty vivid imagination, but I wasn't sure how my body could physically handle them all at once.

"Honestly, we don't know," Leo said. "The curse wasn't exactly specific and it was so long ago we could be mis-remembering."

He looked to the others, who both offered slow nods to some sort of silent question. Leo stepped closer and took my hand, raising it to his chest. His skin was firm and warm underneath my hand, his heart a steady beat.

"It's been a long and certainly shocking day. We aren't going to press you for anything tonight, or ever. So maybe get ready for bed and we'll talk about it more tomorrow." Leo's voice was sincere, patient even.

It was sweet, thoughtful and reasonable. It was definitely the option I should take. But I was orgasm drugged, horny and my pussy ached to be filled again. I had three sexy men wanting to fuck me, so why should I go to bed and handle myself when they could do it for me?

"How about we start with one at a time and see if that breaks your curse? No offense but I don't particularly want any of you in my ass."

Markus took the invitation for what it was. He stepped forward and wrapped a hand around the back of my neck, using his thumb to force my gaze up to his. He dragged the callused digit across my skin and my mouth opened on a gasp.

"Don't worry, pet." He shifted his hand to my throat so he could press his thumb against my bottom lip and slide it into my mouth. It shouldn't have been sexy, but somehow was. He pressed the pad of his thumb against my tongue. "You'll take whatever we give you and you'll be begging for more."

I bit the thumb in my mouth. He hissed out a breath and removed it but only grinned at me.

The hand pressed against Leo's chest was moved lower to rest against his abs. I jerked my gaze over to him. His eyes were dark with want. He leaned forward and kissed me, his tongue going deep as Markus angled me better for him. My head spun with the taste of him.

"As fun as it could be to do this in the hallway, maybe we should take this to the bedroom," Julian suggested.

I started and jerked away from the other two. I had all but forgotten he was there.

How could I do this? There were too many people and limbs and so, so much penis. It was just too much. I looked between them frantically, trying to figure out the logistics of this and just couldn't. I mean, I could imagine it, I'd read enough smut to know exactly what it could look like. But it wasn't anything I'd ever been interested in before.

"Oh, no you don't." Markus hauled me off my feet and threw me over his shoulder. He stalked down the short hall to my bedroom. "You're not going to start panicking now. Don't worry, pet, we'll take it easy on you. And you'll feel so good."

He dropped me on the bed and before I was even done bouncing on the old mattress, he was on top of me. He was so tall, so big. He completely overwhelmed me. Especially when he dropped his mouth to mine. While Leo had explored my mouth, Markus devoured. He took my mouth with lips and teeth and tongue. Licking and nipping at my mouth even as he drew my leg up his side until he was laying between my legs with my core pressed against his belly.

Because of his height, there was no way for our bodies to line up and for him to keep up his assault on my mouth, but suddenly any shyness I had was gone. And all I wanted was to feel that impossibly large dick between my legs. I wriggled against him, looking for friction.

"That's it, pet. Take what you need." Markus whispered against my mouth before pulling back a bit so Julian could tilt my head up and to the right to press his lips to mine. His kiss was softer than both of the others, sweet and slow. Exactly what I'd come to expect from him.

A hand slid up my left arm before sliding between my body and Markus' to cup and knead my breast. My hips jerked and slid against Markus' torso at the unexpected movement. I was still kissing Julian, but I couldn't stop the small whine that escaped me when Markus pulled away.

"It's okay, sweetheart. We've got you," Leo said from my left. His hand abandoned my breast long enough to tug the blanket open and expose me to them again. "Perfection."

A mouth brushed across my nipple and I turned to see Julian's lowered head as he pressed kisses across my skin. Markus leaned down and pressed a kiss to my stomach just above my belly button.

I fought the urge to suck in and make myself seem smaller. They'd all seen me naked already. Two of them had been inside of me. They knew what I looked like. But the old hurts still had their grip on me. I still had a hard time accepting these men wanted me for anything other than breaking their curse.

"Relax, pet," Markus said against the curve of my belly.

"We've got you," Julian said, turning my attention back to him. "Just let us make you feel good." His mouth was back on mine, taking the kiss deeper.

Leo's mouth closed around my nipple and he sucked gently. Markus kissed his way up my thigh. Julian's hand cupped my breast, kneading the abundant flesh before rolling my nipple between his fingers. He slid his hand further down, using two fingers to open my lower lips. Before I could react to that, Markus was there.

I arched into his mouth as he closed over my pussy in a long, wet kiss. Someone's hand went to my belly and pushed me back down, holding me in place. All the while, Julian kept teasing my mouth and Leo was sucking and nipping at my breasts like he'd never get enough.

The sensations were so overwhelming I could no longer tell who was touching me where. But when a finger pressed into me, it could have been no one but Markus. The size of the finger alone gave it away as he stretched me.

"Oh! Oh my god!" I pulled away from Julian's mouth to throw my head back. My hips shifted uselessly under the hands holding me down. Markus had one on my thigh, holding me wide open for him. Julian had one on my belly, pressing me into the bed. Leo's were both distracted with my boobs.

"That's it, dove," Julian said, pressing kisses to my shoulder and neck. "Doesn't it feel good? Markus has a big mouth but thankfully he's good at using it for something other than running his mouth all the time."

There was knowledge in that sentence that tightened my stomach. I pictured Julian with Markus on his knees before him, taking him deep.

"Oh, she likes the idea of us together." Markus said from between my legs. "The way she just clenched around my finger. Mmm."

"Would you like that, sweetheart? Do you want

to watch Markus swallow my cock? He's so good at it. Almost as good at taking cock as he is at eating pretty pussies like yours." Julian's words were filthy and had me panting under their grasping hands. I couldn't catch enough breath.

"Leo's not as good at sucking cock as Markus, or I, but oh, does he love to take it. He's almost always ready to go.

In case I had any doubt about what Julian meant, Markus chose that moment to take the finger from my pussy and press it against my rear entrance.

I clenched and tensed. Markus didn't enter me but kept the circling pressure on the tight hole. Leo abandoned my boobs to whisper in my ear just loud enough for the others to hear.

"You can't imagine how good it feels to get fucked in the ass. To have someone slide into that forbidden entrance. It's so tight and the pressure is so intense. Markus can hit this place so deep that it makes my eyes roll up in my head and breathing next to impossible." He pinched a nipple so hard it was just the right side of pain.

"Can't," I panted. It was all too much. And when Markus bent his head back to my pussy and began sucking and licking my clit in earnest, I was done for. My entire body was a vibrating string, just begging to break.

"I can't," I whined again. It was all too much and not enough, and everything was happening so fast. Markus sucked in my clit at the same time he pushed his broad finger deep into my ass. I clenched and arched, not sure if I wanted more or needed him to stop. Leo returned to sucking and biting at my nipple. Julian turned my head and reclaimed my mouth in a deep, scorching kiss.

The hand on my belly pressed down at the same time Markus moved his free hand from my thigh to my pussy, sliding two fingers deep. And I was lost. I came on a scream as the overwhelm of sensations all hit at once. Every muscle in my body practically vibrated before going tight.

"Fuck, yes, just like that." Julian said, biting my neck behind my ear. "Fuck, dove, I can't wait to get inside of you again."

"You're so fucking sexy," Leo said, abandoning my boobs again to turn my head to kiss me. "That's it lamb, come on Markus' tongue. Mmm. You taste so sweet. Give Markus a taste."

Markus didn't say anything, but his hum vibrated against my pussy and had my legs slamming closed around his head and shoulders. It was so much. Too much. But when Markus pulled his fingers out of me, there was a strange sense of emptiness and loss.

The three men petted and kissed me all over as I came down from my orgasm. They kept their voices soft as they showered me with praise until I lay on the bed like a limp rag.

"That's our good girl," Leo said. "Are you ready for more?"

nine

. . .

ore? What the fuck did he mean more? Every muscle and bone in my body had melted into a giant puddle of girl-shaped goo.

"I think we did her in," Markus said. His voice was smug as he climbed up my body to press a kiss to my lips. "Be gentle with her."

I opened my eyes long enough to see his fine ass walk out of my bedroom and into the bathroom right across the hall. I looked back to Leo, who grinned at me.

"Don't look too sad, lamb. He'll be back. He's had his turn with that sweet cunt. He'll get cleaned up while Julian and I take our turns." He pressed a kiss to my lips. "I want to try something, are you up for that?"

I glanced over to Julian, who grinned down at me and pressed another kiss to my shoulder. It was then that I realized he'd crawled onto the bed with me, his hard cock pressed against my leg. I must have been really distracted to not notice that.

Leo was kneeling on the ground on the other

side of my low-profile queen bed. The position put him at the perfect height to nuzzle my breasts. The man seemed obsessed with my boobs.

"If you're about to suggest fucking my tits, the answer is no."

Leo laughed and buried his face in my boob.

"No, little lamb. As good as that would be, that's not what I'm thinking. Can you move up the bed?" I was still laying with my legs hanging over the end. I took a quick assessment and decided I could manage wiggling up the mattress.

"That's a good girl," Julian said, pressing a kiss to my neck. "Leo's going to fuck you now, okay? He's going to slide his cock into your pretty pussy and you're going to take all of him."

Leo got to his feet, putting his cock right above me. He wasn't as long as Julius, or as overall large as Markus, but there was nothing small about the man. He caught me looking and grinned, stroking his hand over his cock in a slow stroke that had me tightening my thighs. Oh yeah, I was going to take him.

"What are you going to be doing?" I asked Julian. "Because Leo fucking my pussy isn't anything worth writing home about."

Julian barked out a laugh, and Leo made an affronted, huffing sound. I played back my words and cringed. Looking back to Leo, I explained.

"Your penis is very pretty and I enjoyed it very much. But that's pretty tame. Not sure it was worth the build up."

"Julian is going to get your ass ready." Leo's hand slid under me to squeeze the round globes of it. "Trust me, you'll want him in your ass. For the first time, anyway. He's not quite as wide as I am and neither of us have anything on Markus. You'll have to work your way up to us."

I bit my lower lip and considered them. I'd never had a cock in my ass before. I've never done more than a finger or two. And while Julian's cock wasn't as wide as the others, it didn't mean he didn't have a pretty significant package.

"Nothing you don't like, remember?" Julian's words were soft against my shoulder. "Just say stop and we stop. But you're the only one who can free us and we need to try. Please."

"Please," Leo echoed.

After a long moment, I nodded. I'd told them I'd help, and I wanted to. Part of me was curious about it. If it didn't kill me, it could be the best sex I'd ever had. How would I ever live with the regrets if I didn't take full advantage of the situation?

"Okay, how do we do this?" Leo's grin was downright wolfish as he climbed onto the end of the bed and up until his hips were cradled between my thighs.

"First, I'm going to fuck you. And you're going to like it." And with that, he pushed inside of me in one hard thrust. I cried out, sensitive and overstimulated and oh, so full.

"You will, you know," Julian said beside my ear. His hand cupped and kneaded my breast. "Leo knows just how to use that cock of his."

I could barely focus on him as Leo kept up a slow, brutal pace. My legs were braced on his hips as he moved in and out of me, and they shook with every movement. My body was wound tight and on the verge of breaking when Leo stopped moving and rolled us until I was on top.

"Are you ready, lamb? Julian's going to join us."

"Not yet." We all stopped and looked over as

Markus walked back into the room. He'd cleaned his face and brushed through his hair. He was so tall, big, and hard. So impossibly hard.

"Oh, she likes you," Leo said with a sly grin. "Her sweet little cunt just about strangled my cock."

I buried my face against his neck to hide my sudden embarrassment. I didn't like Markus. I didn't know him. Sure, he was attractive. All of them were. But there was something about Markus' imposing body and dominant personality that really did it for me. Not that the other two weren't doing it for me. They'd been doing it for me from the second Julian transformed from a train.

Large, callused hands stroked down my back and over my ass before his fingers veed out to surround Leo's cock where it was buried inside of me. Markus cupped my pussy and teased at my clit.

"I think it's my turn, don't you."

I whimpered as he pressed down against my pleasure center with one blunt finger. The whimper turned into a whine when Leo pulled out of me.

"Do you always do what he says?" I asked as Leo helped me maneuver off him.

"Man's got a point. Julian and I have both had a chance to be inside of that sweet little cunt." He held my arms as I dropped to the bed beside him. "Unless you don't want to fuck Markus?"

Of fucking course I wanted to fuck Markus. The man pushed buttons I didn't even know I had. I just wasn't sure how I felt about being manipulated and moved around like a passive participant.

Some of my thoughts must have crossed my face because Leo flashed a grin and leaned forward to lay a smacking kiss on my mouth. He released me and moved off the bed to join Julian on the far side of the room. Both watched with bright eyes as Markus came forward. He crawled onto the bed with more grace than a man his size should have possessed. I watched him come for me with wide eyes.

"Don't worry, love." Markus said, looming over me until I was laying back on the bed again. "You're going to love what we do to you. We're going to ruin you for other men."

I was about to protest when Markus' mouth slammed down onto mine. His tongue brushed against my lower lip before demanding access. He kissed me like I was air, and he was drowning. My head was spinning. I wrapped my arms and legs around him, trying to anchor myself in place.

"Are you ready for me, love?" Markus muttered against my lips.

"Yes," the word was a breath. It was apparently enough because suddenly we were moving. Markus flipped over until he was on his back, he hauled me against his chest and gripped my hips.

"Warn a girl next time!" I was laughing as I settled against his lower stomach. Markus let out a quick grin, an expression that didn't look quite natural on his harsh face. It made it all the more appealing.

"Ride me," he commanded, using his grip on my hips to slide me down and over his cock. I ground against it, enjoying the hard ridge against my moist folds. "Not what I meant, pet."

A warm body pressed against my back and I looked over my shoulder to see Julian there. His arms wrapped around my torso under my breasts and he lifted me up enough for Markus to line his cock up with my opening.

"Slow now," Julian warned as he pressed me

down onto Markus' cock. "We don't want to break that pretty pussy."

Breaking it felt like a possibility. Leo was wide, Julian was long. Markus was both. And more. The stretch felt almost impossible as Julian helped press me down the length of Markus' cock. Markus kept his hands firm on my hips, giving micro thrusts into me as my pussy worked itself open. I'm not sure I would have managed it without their help. It was so much.

I was shaking and near tears by the time I was fully seated on Markus's dick. It was so much more than I'd ever taken.

"That's our good girl," Julian whispered into my hair as he hugged me close. "I know he's a lot but doesn't it feel so good? Isn't it satisfying to know you've got all that dick inside of you and that huge man at your mercy?"

At my mercy? The idea was ridiculous. But then I opened my eyes and focused on Markus' face. His mouth was drawn into a firm line, his thick, dark brows low over his dark eyes. The hands gripping my hips were shaking. He was hanging on by a thread and all I'd done was worked my way down his cock.

I leaned forward, and Julian released me. His hands joined Markus's on my hips. Moving slowly, I ground myself over Markus. It was so much, the pressure against my cervix was bordering on pain. But the more I moved, the better everything felt. I rocked slowly as I adjusted to his size and the hands on my hips tightened and trembled. It was a heady sort of power.

I had just found a slow, grinding rhythm when Julian's hand released my hip. I glanced over at Leo, who just grinned at me as he stood beside the bed, stroking his cock. I wanted to do that for him, but I didn't have the focus or coordination to manage. Especially not when Julian's hand returned to press a damp finger against my ass.

"Oh, fuck." I rocked back, the movement pushed his finger deeper inside of me. "Lube. Lube in the drawer." I waved a hand at the bedside table that housed my toys, cleaner, and lube.

Leo jumped to action, pulling the drawer open and quickly locating the bottle.

"Well, this is handy." He popped the top of the bottle and poured a small amount into his hand. He lifted it to his nose and sniffed the strawberry flavored and scented lubricant. "Smells much better than anything we had."

He handed the bottle to Julian, who removed his digit from me. It only took a moment before his finger was back, this time coated with the lube. He pressed his finger deep, twisting and curling it inside of me. I rocked on Markus' cock as Julian worked my back door open with one, and then two fingers.

It was so intense I wasn't sure how to process the sensations overtaking me. My whole body was trembling nonstop as they continued to fuck me. I could feel Leo's gaze on us and it just made it hotter. I braced myself on Markus's chest with one hand and reached the other out to Leo, needing him to be a part of this.

He took my hand and stepped forward, but made no move to join us on the bed. I let out a whine when Julian added another finger and spread them wide. Leo's grip tightened on mine.

"You're doing so well, little lamb." He brought my hand to his lips to kiss the knuckles in an achingly sweet gesture. "You're almost there."

"Pretty sure I'm too full to come." I muttered, unable to form words. Markus thrust up inside of me at the same time Julian eased his fingers out of me. I gasped and moaned.

"You'll come again," Markus said. "You won't be able to stop yourself once we're all inside of you."

I was about to argue with him when Julian removed his fingers. The loss was keen. At least, it was until the head of Julian's cock pressed against my hole. Just that press was enough to have me tensing up. Was I really doing this?

"Shhh, dove. We'll make it so good for you." Julian whispered in my ear as he pressed inside. Just the head of him was so much. Too much. Overwhelming.

My breath was coming in short pants as I tried to relax around them. I was so impossibly, almost painfully full. Markus held me still against him as Julian pressed deep.

"Oh, fuck. Fuck, fuck, fuck, fuck, fuck." The word was a prayer and a curse. A litany I could not stop chanting as Julian slid the last of his length inside of me and came to stop.

"Still with us, love?" Markus skimmed a hand up my sternum to come to rest around my throat. He didn't press, but the pressure was enough to help slow my breathing from near hyperventilation levels.

I couldn't speak. I just nodded and held myself still as I adjusted to the fullness inside of me. Markus's cock twitched, and I whined.

"Don't move," I panted out. "Wait."

"Forever for you, love." Markus pressed against my throat and used his grip to turn my head toward Leo, who swept in for a kiss. He tangled his hands in my hair and devoured my mouth. My head swam with it all. And that was before the other men started to move.

It started with slow grinds and shallow thrusts, but as Leo kissed me until the top of my head blew off, the other two sped up. They worked together in practiced movements, pulling out and sliding home opposite of each other.

Eventually, I couldn't focus on kissing Leo. I couldn't focus on anything but the overwhelmingly huge feeling inside of me. The pleasure pooling in my stomach was wound so tight it was nearly painful. I shook uncontrollably as they moved.

"Is it my turn yet?" Leo asked. I stared at him with wide eyes, trying to make sense of the question.

"You better do it soon," Markus said, his teeth gritted tight. "She feels so fucking good."

"Hurry," Julian said through gritted teeth. "I'm almost there."

Leo didn't need any more prodding. He climbed onto the bed and straddled Markus' face. His dick was so hard and leaking precum. I licked my lip and waited for him to move close enough for me to wrap my lips around it.

"God, stuffed so full you can barely move and still begging for more." Leo cupped my face and rubbed his thumb against my lower lip. I lapped at it with my tongue. "You are utter perfection."

With that, he released me to grip his dick and leaned forward to ease it into my mouth. He was too wide to do much more than suck it as hard and as deep as I could go. I was filled more than I'd ever been in my entire life. My head buzzed with pleasure and pain and overstimulation.

I didn't do much. I couldn't do much. I was

trapped between the men who were setting the pace for our shared pleasure. I was a tight string of sensation, just waiting to snap. Which is exactly what happened when Julian wrapped an arm around my waist to slide his hand down to rub at my clit.

I screamed. Later, I would be embarrassed by it and how the neighbors had to have heard but in the moment, I was nothing but sensation, and pleasure. The sound was somewhat muffled with the cock in my mouth, but the sound rang through the room.

"That's it, love," Markus crooned. He cupped my breasts and plucked at my tight nipples. "Come for us."

"Fuck, she's perfect." Julian's hand continued to stroke my clit as he continued his slow, steady movements in my ass.

"Do you hear that, lamb? You're perfect. Made just for us. Made to take our cocks, our perfect little lamb." Leo's movements stuttered and his grip in my hair tightened.

It only made the pleasure grow. My eyes rolled up and my breath was mere pants around Leo's dick as I tried to keep it together long enough for them to come. They had to come. I wouldn't survive it much longer, but they had to come.

"Oh fuck," Leo said. He slid a little too deep until my entire body seized up and I gagged around his width. "Yes, fuck. Yes!"

"Gods be damned," Julian said. He abandoned my clit to grip my hips and slam deep. I could feel the throbbing of his cock inside of me as he came.

"Come again for me, love." Markus demanded, thrusting up into me. "I want to feel you come on my cock one more time."

I shook my head. There was no way. No fucking

way I could come again. But when he slid a hand up to grip my neck and the other down to thumb my clit, I shattered. Everything went white with black along the edges.

"Fuuuuuuuck!" Markus roared the word. It was the last thing I heard before everything went dark.

ten

. . .

"Wake up, dove." The masculine voice sounded far away at first, but slowly came into focus. "That's it. Time to open your eyes. Let's get you cleaned up."

Warm arms wrapped around me and lifted me off the bed. I was glad for the assist, because my everything hurt and I wasn't sure if I could stand. I could barely open my eyes.

"Can't move." I muttered against Julian's chest. It shook under me as he chuckled. "Dead."

"Not dead but you did scare the shit out of Leo when you went limp on us." I tried to look around for the other man, but could barely lift my head. "He's in the bathroom."

"Oh. K. Where we going?" My throat was raw and words hurt. Everything felt raw and sore and ached.

"Bathroom. Leo's getting you a bath ready. Markus is raiding your kitchen for some tea or honey." Julian carried me out of the bedroom and across the hall to the bathroom. The room was already steamy and warm. I nearly went boneless at the thought of a nice, hot bath. Maybe I would just live there from then on.

"Is she awake?" Leo's voice was concerned.

I felt bad for scaring him. But really, it was their fault for fucking me senseless. Still, it was their fault. If they hadn't fucked me senseless I wouldn't have passed out. They had no one to blame but themselves.

"Barely. It may have been too much too soon." Julian's voice was worried. "Okay, dove. In we go."

Instead of helping me into the tub as I'd expected, he climbed in and settled with me on his lap. It was kind of nice, cuddling against his hard body with the hot water swirling around us. But my bath wasn't that big and I would have preferred bathing alone. I could have at least sunk into the water then.

"We had a time limit. But I think you're right. We'll have to go easier on her next time." Leo was kneeling on the ground next to the tub. He picked up a cup he'd gotten from the kitchen and filled it with water before dumping it over my hair.

"Next time?" I muttered the words, content to lay against Julian's chest as Leo wet my hair.

"Unless you don't want us." His voice was soft and careful.

Did I want them? Twenty-four hours ago, I didn't know them at all. Twelve hours ago they'd been trains. It was completely insane that I'd had sex with one of them, let alone all three. But at the same time, I felt more cherished and cared for than I had my entire life.

They worshiped me. They cared for me. Even as he waited for my answer, Leo was filling his hand with shampoo to wash my tangled hair. Julian's breath was shallow beneath my head, but he kept his arms tight around me like he could hold me forever.

"Of course she wants us." Markus came into the room carrying a steaming mug and a bottle of water.

And there he was. Mr. Certainty, ready to come in and take over. And yet, the confidence and certainty I would keep them was appealing. Sometimes it was exhausting to always be the one to make decisions. I couldn't let him have his way all the time because he'd become insufferable, but sometimes, it might be nice to let him take charge and decide what's best for all of us.

"Oh, yeah?" My voice was a croak, and I managed to raise my arms enough to accept the steaming mug when Markus shoved it at me.

"Of course. You'd be an idiot to give us up and you're no idiot." He gave me a lopsided grin and set the bottle of water on the counter.

I took a sip of the tea in the mug and sighed. I wasn't much of a tea drinker. The tea I had was more for Cinder than me, but I could admit the warm liquid with a hint of honey was soothing on my sore throat. Combined with Leo's deft fingers scrubbing at my scalp, I couldn't have felt more relaxed.

Maybe keeping them around wouldn't be such a terrible thing. It was completely insane, but not terrible.

"How do I even explain you?" I asked, more to myself than them.

"Tell the truth, we're the fools who worship you." Leo grinned at me, hopeful.

"The men intent on giving you everything you want." Julian tilted my head until he could press a sweet kiss to my lips.

"How about the men who fuck you so well you pass out?" Markus suggested. I glanced over Leo's head where he was leaning against the counter with his arms crossed. Still naked, still so confident in himself and his body.

"We're going to need a bigger bed." I muttered.

"We'll figure it out." Markus promised. And I believed him. Was it crazy? Yes. Absolutely. I had no clue how I was going to explain dating three men to my friends and family. Especially not three men I'd never mentioned before, but were now suddenly living with me.

It didn't matter. None of it mattered. I sipped my tea and relaxed against Julian as Leo rinsed the shampoo from my hair.

Yeah, a girl could get used to that.

epilogue

. . .

The call Sunday morning asking me to return to the vintage store had come as a surprise to me, but none of the guys seemed particularly shocked. They also insisted on coming along, which made the trip a whole ordeal.

First, I'd had to go to the supercenter to pick up sweatpants and t-shirts and sneakers for everyone since nothing in my five-two closet was going to fit a single one of the giant men. And since none of them had worn clothing since the Romans invaded England, it had been a guessing game trying to pick sizing. It wasn't like I could haul three naked men to the store with me. Though Leo had tried to convince me a bedsheet toga was acceptable enough.

Then, I'd had to load the three poorly dressed men into my compact sedan to drive across town. And while they'd enjoyed finally seeing the modern world, they'd only sensed from their train prisons, none of us had enjoyed the experience of three six-plus feet men in the tiny car. I felt like a clown car when we finally arrived and found parking in Old Town.

"Adding a large SUV to the list of things we desperately need," I said, more to myself than the men. Something they clearly picked up on because not one replied to me.

I headed toward the store, and the men fell into step around me. Markus wrapped an arm around my waist, Leo around my shoulder. Julian was holding Leo's free hand on the other side. I had to admit, it made having three boyfriends easier when those boyfriends were also boyfriends.

I'd known they'd fucked. They'd said as much. But I hadn't really expected the easy intimacy between them all. Julian and Leo were both very touchy-feely and had no problem showing affection for each other. Markus was somewhat more reserved, but I'd caught him with his hand around Julan's neck and his tongue down the other man's throat that morning.

Their arms all fell away as we reached the door to Retro Whimsey. Julian held it open while Markus ushered me through into the brightly lit store.

"Welcome to Retro Whimsey!" The woman behind the counter wasn't the same one I'd bought the trains from. This girl was younger, with blond hair and bright blue eyes. She was dressed casually in a flowing yellow dress and her hair was braided away from her face. Her face lit up when she saw us.

"Oh! It's you!" Every sentence she spoke ended in an exclamation. It was as annoying as it was endearing. "I'm so glad you came back! And you brought the men! It's so wonderful to see you all. I have something for you!"

She headed into the back through a long black curtain. I could hear her rummaging around back there and wondered what was going on.

"Do you know her?" I asked the guys. All three shook their heads, but all three were focused completely on the curtain the woman had disappeared behind.

"Do we think?" Leo asked. But the woman was back before he could go on. She was carrying a wood box roughly the size of a shoe box.

"This is for you!" She handed the box to me and I slid the lid off. "We converted the currency from your banks into modern funds and put it in an account for you. We had to update some of your information but there's everything you need to survive in the modern world. Do try not to piss off any more gods."

I handed the lid to Julian and shuffled through the box in my arms. There were state IDs, passports, birth certificates, social security cards, and a bank book. I flipped it open and nearly dropped the box.

"That can't be right." I eyed the initial deposit amount listed, the only transaction in the book. I looked between the three men. "That, that… that's."

"Breathe love," Markus said, patting me on the back. "We were exceptionally good at being soldiers. Now we can get that new bed you wanted."

The account held millions. We could buy a new house with the sunken tub I'd been dreaming about since Friday night. A bed big enough to fit the four of us instead of the queen that barely fit three of us. I guess I didn't have to worry about overtime to get the new SUV to fit us all.

I wanted them without the money, but it didn't hurt to know that I wouldn't be going bankrupt trying to clothe and house three giant men.

"Is there anything else I can do for you?" The

woman asked with a bright smile. I noticed the Trogg dolls sitting on the shelf near the counter.

"You know what, I think I'll get a gift for a friend."

"That sounds like a lovely idea!"

about the author

Sabrina Cross (she/her) is a neurospicy 80's baby from the middle of nowhere Michigan, where she still lives with her cat. She came into her monster romance era early when she fell in love with Beast from the 1997's X-Men animated series. After discovering sentient object romance in early 2023, Sabrina decided to embrace what she calls her 'Hold My Beer' style of writing and gave into the lifelong dream of being an author. When not writing weird monster/sentient object smut, Sabrina can be found hanging out on social media (@authorsabrinacross), reading, or hoarding office supplies.

also by sabrina cross

Yarn & Monsters Series

A True Love Spell Gone Wrong...

When four friends perform a true love spell, things go terribly wrong. Now they're locked into a deal with the devil and have only a year to find love and happiness or their souls are destined to face the flames. Armed with a demon guardian; Clover, Jasmine, Fern, and Violet are determined to beat the devil and save themselves. Except, this curse might be the best thing that's ever happened to them.

Corny: A F/F Candy Corn Romance

A True Love Spell Gone Wrong…

A Demon Fairy Godmother?

Her very soul on the line. Can Clover still find true love or is she destined to face the flames alone?

Snuggle: A M/F Demon Teddy Bear Romance

A True Love Spell Gone Wrong…

Jasmine is too busy to go to Hell and she's definitely too busy for demon antics. But when her demon "Fairy Godmother" shows up, everything is on the line. Does she have what it takes to get out of the Devil's bargain or is she doomed to face the flames?

Tangled: A M/F Friends-To-Lovers Sentient Object Romance

A True Love Spell Gone Wrong…

Fern is going to Hell. Not metaphorical Hell but actual, physical Hell. But there's one thing she needs to do before she goes. An item she desperately needs to scratch off the bucket list. And she's hoping the demon sent to guard her will be willing to help her out.

Knotted: A M/F Demon Werewolf Romance

A True Love Spell Gone Wrong...

Violet was no witch but that didn't stop her from trying to use magic to find love. When the spell backfired and left her and her friends bound in a deal with the devil, Violet vowed to find a solution. Now, with less than two months until the deal comes due and zero leads, she's facing the fire. The fire comes early in the form of a great black beast in her bed. Does Violet find the love she's been looking for or does Hell claim her soul?

Light Me Up

He was the first man to ever turn me on. When he flipped my switch and lit me up that first time, I knew he was it for me. There would never be another.

Pounded by the Pommel Horse

Elena loves being on top. When the elite gymnast is challenged to defeat her gym rival on the pommel horse, she's up for the task. But is she up for the ride when the pommel horse shapeshifts into a man? A very, very naked Man?

Christmas with the Monster

He's Got a Package for Her... Devynn expected her first holiday without her kids to be difficult. But nothing could have prepared her for what she found under the tree just after midnight.With the help of his magic sack, the furry, green giant promises Devynn all kinds of pleasure. But would one night with the Christmas monster ever be enough?

Sentient Pen15 from Outer Space

Liam had spent a lot of his childhood obsessed with the legends of the local mines. The abandoned tunnels underground had driven dozens of workers insane and young Liam was desperate to get to the bottom of it. But he found more than he bargained for down there.

Infected by parasitic space mold, Liam has held himself away from relationships for years. When things spark between him and the girl next door, he has no choice but to reveal the truth: his manly appendage is also the bane of his existence.

The Glory Whole Package

Never Piss Off a Witch.

It is a hard-learned lesson and one I may never complete. The endless boredom of my curse is only broken by analyzing the people who use me.

Today I break my silence for the first time and while it might lead to a Happily Ever After, it will never be mine. Not until I've paid for my crimes and earned the forgiveness of the only person I've ever loved.